W9-AAH-023

Praise for
The Fix-It Friends: Have No Fear!

"Fears are scary! But don't worry: the Fix-It Friends know how to vanquish all kinds of fears, with humor and step-by-step help. Nicole C. Kear has written a funny and helpful series."

—**Fran Manushkin, author of the Katie Woo series**

"Full of heart and more than a little spunk, this book teaches kids that fear stands no chance against friendship and courage. Where were the Fix-It Friends when I was seven years old?"

—**Kathleen Lane, author of *The Best Worst Thing***

"I love the Fix-It Friends as a resource to give to the families I work with. The books help kids see their own power to overcome challenge—and they're just plain fun to read."

—**Lauren Knickerbocker, PhD, Co-Director, Early Childhood Clinical Service, NYU Child Study Center**

"Hooray for these young friends who work together; this diverse crew will have readers looking forward to more."

—*Kirkus Reviews*

The Fix-It Friends

Eyes on the Prize

Nicole C. Kear
illustrated by Tracy Dockray

【Imprint】
MAKE YOUR MARK

NEW YORK

[Imprint]
MAKE YOUR MARK

A part of Macmillan Publishing Group, LLC
175 Fifth Avenue, New York, NY 10010

THE FIX-IT FRIENDS: EYES ON THE PRIZE. Text copyright © 2018 by
Nicole C. Kear. Illustrations copyright © 2018 by Imprint. All rights reserved. Printed
in the United States of America by LSC Communications, Harrisonburg, Virginia.

Library of Congress Cataloging-in-Publication Data

Names: Kear, Nicole C., author. | Dockray, Tracy, illustrator.
Title: The fix-it friends: eyes on the prize / Nicole C. Kear ; illustrated by Tracy Dockray.
Other titles: Eyes on the prize
Description: First edition. | New York : Imprint, 2018. | Series: The Fix-It Friends ; [5] |
    Summary: The Fix-It Friends help Matt, Veronica's annoying classmate, get organized
    after she is teamed with him for a 100 Day assignment. Includes notes for children and
    their parents. | Includes bibliographical references.
Identifiers: LCCN 2017031964 (print) | LCCN 2017004965 (ebook) |
    ISBN 9781250086730 (Ebook) | ISBN 9781250115805 (hardcover) |
    ISBN 9781250086723 (pbk.)
Subjects: | CYAC: Cooperativeness—Fiction. | Orderliness—Fiction. | Helpfulness—
    Fiction. | Brothers and sisters—Fiction. | Friendship—Fiction. | Schools—Fiction.
Classification: LCC PZ7.1.K394 (print) | LCC PZ7.1.K394 Eye 2018 (ebook) |
    DDC [Fic]—dc23
LC record available at https://lccn.loc.gov/2017031964

Our books may be purchased in bulk for promotional, educational, or business use.
Please contact your local bookseller or the Macmillan Corporate and Premium
Sales Department at (800) 221-7945 ext. 5442 or by e-mail at
MacmillanSpecialMarkets@macmillan.com.

Book design by Ellen Duda
Illustrations by Tracy Dockray
Imprint logo designed by Amanda Spielman

First edition, 2018

ISBN 978-1-250-11580-5 (hardcover)

1 3 5 7 9 10 8 6 4 2

ISBN 978-1-250-08672-3 (trade paperback)

1 3 5 7 9 10 8 6 4 2

ISBN 978-1-250-08673-0 (ebook)

mackids.com

Why You Shouldn't Steal This Book
by Jude Conti

1. It's unethical. Like, just plain wrong.
2. You'll get caught.
3. You don't need to! It's basically the whole reason libraries were invented.

For my mother and father,

who've always paid attention

Special thanks to Cindy Goldrich, EdM,

author of 8 Keys of Parenting Children with ADHD,

for her help as an expert consultant

Chapter 1

My name's Veronica Conti and I love contests.

Staring contest? Sign me up.

Arm-wrestling contest? Yee haw!

Eating contest? I'm your girl . . . unless I have to eat broccoli. Or cauliflower. Or arugula. I have never tried arugula, but the name sounds gross. Ar-uguuuuuu-la.

I love contests. Sometimes you win, and sometimes you lose, and it's fun either way.

But it's more fun if you win. Especially if you win a trophy.

Trophies! Glorious, golden, gleaming trophies! You put them on your shelf, and they sit there shouting, *Hear ye! Hear ye! This person is a winner!*

At least, I think they do that. I don't know for sure, because I, Veronica Conti, have never won a trophy.

Yes, that's right. I've been alive almost eight years, and I have won zero trophies.

What makes it even worse is that everyone else in my family has one!

My big brother, Jude, is only two years older than me, and he has loads of trophies! He won them for chess championships, drawing competitions, sand-castle contests, and other stuff, too. He has so many trophies, they don't all fit on the shelf above his desk. So Dad had to put up *another* shelf for the extras. How greedy can you get?

Eyes on the Prize

Jude is soooooo proud of his trophies. He polishes them every month. Just to make sure he doesn't forget, he writes *Polish trophies* on the calendar hanging by his desk, on the last Sunday of every month. Once I tried to touch one of his trophies, just to see how it felt, and he snapped, "Get your grubby hands off!"

"I'm the only person who doesn't have a trophy," I complained to Mom. "Jude has too many to count. Cora has three for spelling bees. Ezra has two for robotic contests. Minnie has a whole matching set from piano recitals. Even Matthew Sawyer has a trophy from the science fair last year! For a project called Fantastic Phlegm! And it's not even fair, because his mom helped him and she's a doctor. So of course he won!!"

"It matters not if you win or lose, but how you play the game," Mom replied.

Easy for her to say! She's got a bunch of trophies!

Okay, not trophies exactly. Mom has plaques, which are basically just flattened trophies that hang on the wall. She got them in college, and they're in Latin so I have no idea what they say. For all I know, she got them for winning spitting contests.

Eyes on the Prize

Even my dad has trophies from when he was a basketball star in high school.

When I complained to him, Dad said, "You're not the only one in the family without a trophy. Pearl doesn't have one, either."

"Well, that doesn't count!" I replied. "She's only two years old!"

And then something totally impossible happened.

Pearl got a trophy.

Chapter 2

Technically, what Pearl brought home from day care was a medal and not a trophy. But what's the difference, really? They are both golden and special and prove you're a champion.

Jude and I were in our room, getting ready to do our homework after school. Jude was sitting at his desk, sharpening all his pencils to perfect points. I was lying on my bed, putting kitten stickers on my math notebook because the notebook looked a little boring and because I didn't feel like starting my work.

Eyes on the Prize

I heard the sound of footsteps on the stairs, and then Pearl burst into our bedroom, with Mom right behind her. Pearl was holding her favorite stuffed rat, Ricardo, in one hand and a shiny golden thing in the other hand.

Ricardo looked different. Here's why: He was wearing a pair of Pearl's underwear. It was pink with bunnies all over it. Even though Pearl's underwear is itsy-bitsy, it was still humongous

on Ricardo, so somebody had made it tighter with a safety pin.

Ricardo has been dragged around everywhere with Pearl since she turned two. He had already lost his whiskers and pretty much all his dignity. But he had a tiny shred of dignity left . . . until the bunny panties.

"Wook, Wonny!" said Pearl. She shoved her medal in my hand. "Wook! So pwetty!"

When I saw that medal, I felt two things:

1. Super jealous.

2. Super confused.

Because the medal had a picture of a toilet on it.

"Is this some kind of joke?" I whispered to Mom.

"It's something new the day care is trying, to encourage the kids to use the potty," explained Mom.

Eyes on the Prize

Mom and Dad had been trying to toilet train Pearl for a few months. They even got her a little potty that played music when you sat on it. The song it played was really fast and really loud and totally hilarious.

When Pearl first got it, Jude and I spent about an hour taking turns sitting on the potty—with our pants on, of course—so it would play the song. It went like this:

When you really have to go
Here's what you need to know:
Going potty is so fun
In the rain or in the sun!
Just don't forget to wipe
When you don't wear a diape-
Rrrrrrrrrrrrr!
It's potty time!

It's potty time!

It's potty time!

It's potty time!

"It's the worst song ever!" I laughed.

"Who rhymes *wipe* with *diaper*? It's terrible!"
Jude cackled.

After an hour, though, the song started to get a
little annoying. After a day, it started to get really
annoying. And after a few weeks, it drove us so crazy
that Dad tried to take out the batteries. But it

turned out you couldn't take the batteries out. And there was no off switch.

The worst part was how that annoying song kept getting stuck in all of our heads. So even when Pearl wasn't sitting on the potty, one of us would start singing, "Just don't forget to wipe . . ." and then someone else would shriek, "NOOOOOO! Not the potty song!" and the person would stop singing. But it would be too late, because the song would already be stuck in our heads.

I guess they had a potty at day care, too, because there Pearl stood, showing off her potty medal.

I tried to be happy for Pearl. But now I was the only person in the whole family who didn't have a trophy. It was too much!

"I've never gotten an award for going to the toilet!" I grumbled to Mom as Pearl ran out of the room. "Do you have any idea how many times I've gone? Like, a thousand!"

"Oh, it's way more than that," Jude piped up. He was emptying out his pencil shavings. "Let's say you go to the bathroom an average of six times a day—that's forty-two times a week, which is . . . about 160 times a month. So that would be—" He squinted one eye closed. "That's about 2,000 times a year, and you're almost eight, so . . . you've gone to the toilet 16,000 times."

He snapped his pencil sharpener closed.

"Roughly," he said.

Jude's in fourth grade, so he knows how to multiply and divide and also how to show off.

"See?" I said to Mom. "I have gone to the bathroom 16,000 times! But guess how many toilet medals I have?

"Zero?" asked Mom.

Eyes on the Prize

"That is correct! Zero!"

At that moment, Pearl ran back into our room, wearing nothing but a pair of red socks.

"I'm so big!" she announced. "I did peepee!"

"You did peepee in the potty?" Mom asked.

"No," said Pearl. "On the fwoor! Come see!"

She ran out and Mom followed her, sighing.

"I thought for sure I'd get a trophy for being the president of the Fix-It Friends," I grumbled to Jude. "I save lives, for crying out loud!"

"You're not the president," Jude said. "And you don't save lives. You help kids solve problems."

"What's the difference?" I snapped.

"And," he went on, "if you do ever get a trophy for being a Fix-It Friend, then I should get one, too—and Ezra and Cora. Because we do just as much work as you. We all work together when someone at school has a problem."

He tidied some piles of papers on his desk before opening up his homework folder.

"If you really want a trophy that much, do a great job on your 100 Days project," Jude said. "My class just started working on ours today."

I jumped off my bed and threw my arms around good old Jude.

"Yes! Yes! The 100 Days contest! Of course! You're a genius!"

Every year, in February, my school has a big celebration on the one hundredth day of school. The teachers tell us how proud they are that we've been working so hard for one hundred whole days.

I'm no dummy. I know the real reason the school has a 100 Days celebration. It's a way of tricking us into doing math. They try to make it so much fun that we don't even notice we're learning stuff. Like when Dad puts broccoli in the blender and tries to sneak it into my scrambled eggs. I can always sniff out the broccoli and the math, too. They don't fool me!

But the 100 Days contest is pretty fun, so I don't mind. All the kids work in groups, and you can do absolutely anything you want. Well, not *anything*. The project cannot include:

1. Live animals.

2. Dead animals.

3. Acrobatics.

I found that out the hard way.

But, besides that, you can do whatever you want. The only rule is that it has to include one hundred of something.

Then, on the one hundredth day of school, each grade has a big 100 Days gallery with all the projects, and the students vote for the one they like best.

Here is the important part. Each person in the winning group gets a big trophy. Jude has two of them, from second and third grade. They have a base of pure marble with a big golden *100* on top. They are glorious!

When Jude reminded me about the 100 Days contest, I decided right then and there that I would be the winner for the second grade. I would win that trophy.

After all, if Matthew Sawyer could win a trophy, how hard could it be?

Chapter 3

That Monday, Miss Mabel announced that we were starting our 100 Days projects, just as Jude had predicted. I was super excited and just a little worried about who would be in my group.

Miss Mabel doesn't let us pick our own groups, because she says it causes too much drama. This is the only thing I don't like about her . . . well, this and how she makes us meditate sometimes. Everything else about Miss Mabel is marvelous.

I don't know exactly how old Miss Mabel is, because my mom said it's rude to ask, but she looks really young, almost like a teenager. She isn't married and doesn't have kids. Instead, she has a roommate and two black cats named Trick and Treat. Mabel is her first name, and she lets us call her that because her last name is very long and hard to say. It starts with a *y* and has four *i*'s and three *l*'s and three *a*'s in it.

This is what makes her my BTF (Best Teacher Forever):

1. She plays music for us while we work. Miss Mabel says music is like fertilizer for your brain— it helps ideas grow. Miss Mabel has a lot of cool music on her phone. She used to play it through a little speaker on her desk, but that speaker

stopped working just after the holiday break. I have no proof, but I suspect Matthew Sawyer. I always suspect Matthew Sawyer.

2. She lets us dance to doo-wop. Sometimes school gets so boring, and it's hard to pay attention because it sounds like the teacher is just saying "So you blah blah blah blah blah, and then you blah-de-blah-de-blah, and finally, you just blaaaaaaaaaaaaaah." When school gets this boring, we just talk or horse around. Instead of getting mad at us, Miss Mabel plays a really fast, old-timey song called "Rama Lama Ding Dong." We stand up and dance in our spots like crazy until the song

is over. After that, it's easier to pay attention.

3. She has the best outfits. Grown-ups usually wear super-boring colors like black or brown or gray and hardly any patterns. But Miss Mabel wears bright clothes with flowers or zigzags or even animals on them. She sort of looks like a beautiful, bright piñata. It is exactly the way I want to dress when I am a grown-up.

That Monday afternoon when Miss Mabel announced the groups for the 100 Days project, she looked extra great. She was wearing green corduroy pants with red boots and a button-down shirt that had swans all over it!

Eyes on the Prize

"Your attention, please!" she said in a funny voice, like she was the ringmaster of a circus.

Then she told us to get our math notebooks out, so we could take notes for our 100 Days projects.

I looked in my desk, but I couldn't find my notebook anywhere. Just as I was about to tell Miss Mabel that I didn't have it, I heard a huge crash. Whose desk was it coming from? Take one guess.

Matthew Sawyer's, of course.

Matthew Sawyer is like a pebble in my shoe. Every year, he is in my class, and every year, he drives me bonkers. Here's how:

1. He grosses me out.

2. He plays dumb.

3. He copies me.

4. Other ways that are too many to even count.

The huge crash was the sound of absolutely everything sliding out of Matthew Sawyer's desk. It was an avalanche! Out fell papers and books and broken pencils and dried-up glue sticks and dried-up markers and granola-bar wrappers and winter gloves and hats and dirty tissues. There was even a whole carton of mushrooms in the

pile. Why would someone have a carton of mushrooms in their desk?

In the middle of the pile was a math notebook.

"Just what I was looking for." He grinned. But when he picked it up, he frowned. "Ugh, kittens! This isn't mine!"

I recognized a sticker of a tabby cat wearing an astronaut helmet.

"Hey, that's *mine*!" I said. I marched over and grabbed it out of his hands.

"Stop taking my stuff!" I whispered to him, so Miss Mabel wouldn't hear.

"Why would I want a dumb notebook covered with disgusting kittens?" He made a grimace. "*You* stop leaving your stuff on my desk."

"I would rather leave my notebook in a volcano than—" I started to say, but then Miss Mabel walked over, so I piped down and went back to my desk.

Miss Mabel helped him shove all the stuff back into his desk and asked him, "Did you forget your notebook at home again?"

Matthew Sawyer rubbed his head, which is what he does when he is nervous. He has a buzz cut, so his brown hair is very short. It looks like it would feel fuzzy and soft, but I will never know because I will never, ever in a billion years touch Matthew Sawyer's head.

"I guess I left it in my room," he said. His face got red like he was embarrassed. "Sorry."

He's so forgetful that he'd lose his teeth if they weren't stuck to his gums. Practically the whole Lost and Found belongs to him. There should be a sign on it that says: PROPERTY OF MATTHEW SAWYER.

Miss Mabel told him to just use a piece of loose-leaf paper. Then she read the list of kids in group one and two and three and four and even five. My name wasn't called. I was beginning to think she had forgotten about me when she said, "Last but not least, in group six, we've got Veronica, Cora, Minnie, and—hold on, I can't read my own handwriting here."

As Miss Mabel squinted, trying to see what she had written, Cora and Minnie and I clapped our hands in delight.

Not only are Minnie and Cora my two closest friends, but also they are both great students. Cora is an absolute math whiz! With them in my group, I knew I'd get the trophy for sure. I was so happy, I was bouncing up and down in my seat.

Then Miss Mabel read the name of the last member of our group.

I instantly stopped bouncing. In fact, I felt like my butt had turned into a block of concrete.

The Fix-It Friends

I wanted to grab the sides of my face with my hands and howl, "Noooooooooooooo!"

The name she read was *Matthew Sawyer*.

Chapter 4

As everyone met with their 100 Days groups, I walked over to Miss Mabel. Her wavy black hair was swept up into a bun with a pencil stuck in, to hold it in place.

I think this is the coolest hairstyle ever. Not only does it look great, but also it's useful, too! You always have a pencil when you need one.

"I love your pencil bun," I told Miss Mabel.

"Thanks, lady." She smiled. "What's up?"

"I think there may have been a tiny mistake," I said. "I can't work with Matthew Sawyer."

At just that moment, Matthew Sawyer appeared next to me and said, "Yeah, we can't be in the same group."

Miss Mabel crossed her arms. She looked from me to him and then at me again.

"Kids, I'm disappointed by this," she said. "You haven't even given the collaboration a try."

It feels absolutely terrible when Miss Mabel's disappointed in you. It feels worse than having to do homework on the weekend when everyone else is making ice-cream sundaes.

I gulped hard and nodded. Matthew Sawyer stared at the floor and mumbled, "Sorry."

"Part of the point of this project is to learn how to work together," Miss Mabel said. "I'm here to help. But you've got to give it your best shot."

Then she patted us on our backs and sent us to the rug to work with our group.

Eyes on the Prize

As we walked over, Matthew Sawyer said to me, "I love your shirt."

"Really?" I was surprised because Matthew Sawyer has never, in three years, ever given me one compliment. But I was wearing my favorite shirt, with a picture of a black cat and the words *Meow's It Going?* in a talk bubble coming out of the cat's mouth.

"Thanks!" I said to him. "I like *your* shirt. It's so, so . . ." I tried to think of a compliment

about it, but he was just wearing the same kind of striped shirt he always wears, every single day. "So stripy!"

Matthew Sawyer nodded.

"And yours has a cat on it," he said. "Cats are my favorite."

"I thought you hated cats," I said. "Because they eat bugs and bugs are your favorite."

"I hate bugs! They're the worst. I also hate recess and summer vacation and my birthday. And I am so, so, so happy to be in your group."

I was totally bewildered. Then he started to cackle and said, "And it is definitely *not* opposite day!"

I was so shocked, my jaw dropped open.

"Which means it *is* opposite day!" I cried.

"I'm not saying that."

"Which means you *are* saying that!"

Eyes on the Prize

Matthew Sawyer grinned a wicked grin, just like a wolf. Well, if he was the Big, Bad Wolf and I was a little pig, I would not be one of those blockheaded pigs who made its house out of straw or sticks. I'd be the clever one that made wolf stew at the end.

I leaned in close to him and whispered, "Matthew Sawyer, if you make me lose this trophy, you are going to regret it. If you think I'm kidding, think again. I know kung fu. And my dad has a chain saw."

"I'm t-t-terrified," Matthew Sawyer pretended to stammer. But he only said that because it was opposite day.

Well, fine, I thought. *Two can play at this game.*

"This is going to be great!" I said, gritting my teeth. "Best group ever."

Chapter 5

The good news is, everyone in our group had a ton of ideas for the 100 Days project.

The bad news is, they were all terrible!

Matthew Sawyer's ideas were gross.

"We could do a hundred burps," he said

"Are you saying that because it's opposite day?" I asked him.

"No." He snorted. "Opposite day is so *childish*. Grow up, would you?"

Cora wanted to make a necklace with one hundred beads, and Minnie wanted to write a song with one hundred musical notes. They were both perfectly fine ideas. But they didn't have one iota of pizzazz.

I came prepared, of course: "We'll find a person who is a hundred years old—maybe Mrs. Mackenzie, Principal Powell's secretary. She looks about a hundred. And then she can wink a hundred times or stand on one leg for one hundred seconds or— oh! I know! She can bring in a one-hundred-dollar bill!"

"You're talking about Mrs. Rose," squeaked Cora. She has a high voice that sounds like a hedgehog talking. "But she's not one hundred. She's seventy-one."

Cora knows everything about the grown-ups at our school because they think she's super cute and they love to chat with her. This is one of the reasons she makes such a good Fix-It Friend. I was about to ask her if she could find out how old

Miss Mabel was when I heard Miss Mabel make an announcement.

"Guys, don't forget to break your project down into small steps," she said. "Your final project's due on the hundredth day of school, which is next Thursday. But I want you to give yourself due dates before that for each step."

"Ugh," I groaned. "There's so much to do! We need to think, think, think!"

Cora pulled on her red curls, which is what she does when she is concentrating.

Minnie bit the top of her pencil. She's a think-and-chew-er. When she chews on the ends of her braids, I wag my finger and say, "*¡Comer cabello humano es malo para la digestión!*" which cracks us up. It means "Eating human hair is bad for the digestion" in Spanish. Minnie taught me how to say it. She has taught me all the Spanish I know.

Eyes on the Prize

When I need to think, I tap my fingers. The harder I have to think, the faster I tap. That's just my system.

But of course, Matthew Sawyer snapped at me, "That tapping is distracting me! Cut it out!"

He was busy scribbling on his loose-leaf paper. It looked like he was hard at work. For a second, I thought maybe I was wrong about him. Then I peered over to see what he was writing, and it was just his name over and over again.

"Would you pay attention!" I exclaimed.

"I *am* paying attention! Doodling helps me."

I snorted. "Nice try, Matthew Sawyer."

"Do you have to say my whole name every time? Can't you just call me Matt like everyone else?"

I was about to tell him some other names I could call him that were a lot less nice, but I heard Miss Mabel call out, "I'm seeing a lot of grim faces. Do we need to doo-wop?"

Everyone said, "Yes!" so she put on "Rama Lama Ding Dong." Or she tried to, at least. Without the speaker, the sounds of everyone dancing drowned out the soft music. So halfway through the song, she turned it off and we sat back down.

"I know!" Cora squeaked. "How about we glue one hundred sequins onto something?"

Minnie and I gave each other worried looks.

Eyes on the Prize

"It's a good idea," Minnie said, "but when you were in charge of gluing sequins on the costumes for the play, you, umm . . ."

Matt finished her sentence: "You went totally overboard."

"That's not true!" Cora protested. Her big brown eyes were open wide.

"Cora," Minnie said. "You tried to glue sequins on the piano I was playing."

"You know how, if you give a goldfish too much food, it gobbles all the food up and its stomach gets so overstuffed, it dies?" Matt asked Cora. "That's how you are with sequins."

I glared at Matt. "Why don't we write the idea down as a maybe? It does have razzle-dazzle. But I still think we need something bigger to win the trophy. We need something never seen before! Something that will knock people's socks off!"

Suddenly, Matt gasped. "I have it!" He leaned over and whispered, "What's something everyone has but you don't usually find in one place?"

"Toothbrushes?" asked Minnie.

"Teddy bears?" asked Cora.

"Hot dogs?" I asked.

"Nope," said Matt. "Boogers!"

"If you don't cut it out, I'm going to give you one hundred kicks!" I exclaimed. "And for crying out loud, stop doodling your signature!"

All of a sudden, he did stop.

"Hey, that's it!" he exclaimed.

"A hundred kicks?" I asked. "Really? You would let me do that? I do think it is kind of a great idea."

"No, no, no." He shook his head. "One hundred signatures! We'll collect a hundred signatures! It'll be like a petition."

"Huh?" I asked.

Eyes on the Prize

"A petition," he repeated. "People sign their names on a piece of paper to show they agree with whatever the petition says. My stepdad works for an environmental rights organization, and he writes petitions all the time."

Even I had to admit it was a good idea.

We decided we'd make a really long piece of paper with one hundred lines on it, and we'd roll it up into a scroll so it looked old-fashioned. That way, it would be small enough that we could pass it around at lunch and take it home and stuff.

"And when we get all the signatures, we can attach the petition to a big poster board, which we can decorate!" said Minnie.

"With sequins!" squeaked Cora.

"*Maybe* sequins," I said.

By the time math was over, we had finished our schedule. Minnie wrote it down because she has the best penmanship. I think it's because she has such strong fingers from playing piano.

Step 1: Make petition.

Due date: Wednesday

Step 2: Collect 100 signatures.

Due date: next Tuesday

Step 3: Make fabulous poster (maybe with sequins).

Due date: Thursday, the 100th Day of school!

There were more steps that I suggested, but Minnie would not write them down. They were:

Step 4: Accept trophy.

Step 5: Cry for joy.

Step 6: Pause for applause.

Chapter 6

The next day, during math, Miss Mabel called our group to her desk to review our project idea and schedule.

Miss Mabel has all sorts of cool stuff on her desk. She has a timer that's in the shape of an owl, so you don't lose track of time. She also has a basket full of fidgets, which are toys you can fiddle with if you are getting antsy. She also has lots of framed photos.

My favorite is the picture from when Miss Mabel was in second grade, just like me. In the photo, she is at a fancy party with her mom, and she's wearing

the most beautiful outfit I have ever seen. It is purple and silky, with gold around the edges, and it comes in two pieces—a long skirt that reaches to the floor and a matching top that wraps around her body and hangs over her shoulder like a scarf. Her mom is wearing the same kind of outfit, only in orange.

Once I asked her where she got the outfit, and she said, "It's from India. It's a sorry."

"Sorry for what?" I asked.

She laughed. "*S-a-r-i*. It's a traditional kind of clothing in India."

"Well, I am *sorry* I don't have a *sari*," I said. "Do they come in turquoise?"

Eyes on the Prize

On that Tuesday, while Cora explained our project idea to Miss Mabel, I was looking at that picture and daydreaming about how, if I had a sari, I would wear it to accept my trophy at the 100 Days celebration. Maybe Miss Mabel could wear one, too, and we could be twins.

When Cora was done talking, Miss Mabel said, "I love it! It's fresh and new and *very* collaborative."

We all beamed, even Matt.

"Today, you can decide what you're going to write on your petition. It should be something all of you can agree on."

"If there *is* such a thing," I muttered. I didn't think Matt and I would ever agree on anything!

And I was right. We spent most of math time arguing about what the petition should say. While we were in the middle of brainstorming, Matt bent over to look at something on the floor.

"Matt!" I exclaimed. "You're not even paying attention!"

He said "Shhhhhhhh!" without even looking at me.

That got me curious, so I bent over to see what he was looking at.

It was a water bug. They are basically the same as cockroaches, just with a nicer name. Sometimes one will appear in our house, because it's a very old house that was built in the Pilgrim times, or around then. Whenever my grandmother sees a bug, she shrieks at the top of her lungs and stands on a chair. But I'm not scared of bugs, so I just run over and smash it with my shoe for her. Nana is always very grateful and gives me a cookie.

As soon as I saw that water bug, I jumped up and stomped on it.

Eyes on the Prize

"HEY!" Matt shouted. He looked at me with a horrified expression that said, *How could you do such a terrible thing, you heartless monster?*

"What did he ever do to you?" Matt asked very bitterly.

"I was *trying* to help!" I exclaimed. "And if you were paying attention and working on our petition, instead of looking at bugs, this wouldn't have happened!"

"That's not the point!" he cried. "You murdered an innocent creature!"

"He was a gross cockroach!"

"He may have been a cockroach, but he was *not* gross," Matt said in a huff. His eyes were flashing with fury. "You're the gross one."

I was so angry at Matthew Sawyer that I thought I might sock him. So I stood up to get a drink of water and cool off, like my mom always tells me to do.

On my way back to the group, I passed Miss Mabel, who was putting new batteries in her speaker. She pressed the power button, but nothing happened.

"Can't get the speaker to work?" I asked.

"Nope," she said, tossing it in the trash. "It's too bad. Our doo-wops have been a bit lackluster lately."

"Why don't you just ask Principal Powell for a new one?"

"I did," Miss Mabel said. "But speakers cost money, so—"

"Eureka!" I shrieked. Miss Mabel looked at me like I was growing wings out of my ears.

"Sorry, Miss Mabel, it's just . . . I had a great idea! Gotta tell the group."

I raced over to the rug, where Matt was trying to persuade everyone to make a petition that said, "Ban the murder of water bugs! Water bugs are people, too."

"First of all, water bugs are not people," I said. "They're bugs."

Matt opened his mouth to say something, but I stopped him.

"But it doesn't matter, anyway, because I've got the perfect idea!" I exclaimed. "The petition should ask for a new speaker for Miss Mabel! So she can doo-wop again!"

Everyone agreed it was perfect. Minnie wrote the petition in her best handwriting:

"Miss Mabel is the best teacher ever! Please give her a new speaker. She needs it to teach us!"

Finally, we could move on to the fun step: getting signatures. We decided we'd each get to take the petition home for one day.

Petition Schedule

Cora: Wednesday to Thursday

Minnie: Thursday to Friday

Veronica: Friday to Monday

Matt: Monday to Tuesday

I made sure I got the longest turn because I knew I could get a billion signatures if I just had enough time.

I also made sure Matthew Sawyer got the last turn.

Told you I was the clever piggy.

Chapter 7

Cora asked for her signatures very sweetly and got lots of them, especially from the teachers, who cannot resist her. By the time her turn was over, she had gotten seventeen signatures.

Then it was Minnie's turn, and she did a good job, too. She got fifteen signatures.

"I would have gotten more, but my piano lesson last night was extra long," she said. "I have a really big recital in a few days. I have to play allegro!"

"Hey! That's not Spanish; that's Italian!" I said. "It means 'happy.' My grandmother says it sometimes."

"Well, in music it means you have to play really fast, which is really hard," she said. "And right now, it does not make me happy! It makes me stressed out! So I have to have extra lessons to get ready, and I only got fifteen signatures." She stuck the end of her braid in her mouth.

"Minerva Ramos!" I exclaimed. "*¡Comer cabello humano es malo para la digestión!*"

She burst out giggling.

"Don't worry!" Cora said. "We have tons of signatures—thirty-two all together."

Next, it was my turn. I don't mean to brag, but you will never guess how many signatures I got.

Sixty-six.

Yep, that's right.

Sixty-six!

Eyes on the Prize

Want to know my secret? It's easy. Just ask absolutely everyone. Also, don't take "no" for an answer. Also, give away free doughnuts.

I got a bunch of signatures during math time, at recess, and during lunch, too—until Miss Tibbs noticed what I was doing. As soon as she saw my petition, she rolled it right up and put it in her pocket. She said it was "not an appropriate lunchtime activity." Big surprise! According to Miss Tibbs, even laughing is "not an appropriate lunchtime activity." She doesn't know the meaning of *fun*.

I used to think Miss Tibbs was an evil witch like in *The Wizard of Oz* because she wears all black and frowns all the time. Then she gave me a homework pass for helping out a friend who has trouble reading, and I decided she's probably not a witch.

But, even so, she is the strictest teacher I've ever met and definitely a party pooper.

So I was not surprised when she snatched up my petition at lunch. But I *was* surprised when she gave it back to me after lunch, and I noticed she had signed it. Yippee-ki-yay!

On Saturday, Nana and Nonno and Jude and Mom and Dad signed. Even Pearl wanted to sign!

"She can't even write yet!" protested Jude.

I glared at him. "Toddlers are people, too, you know."

Then I put my hand on top of Pearl's hand to help her write her name. It looked pretty messy, but you could still sort of read it.

Right after she finished her signature, she went potty. Except she didn't go *in* the potty. She went on the floor. Right next to my feet!

Eyes on the Prize

"Pearly Pie," I said. "You really have to remember to go into the bathroom."

"When you weally have to go—" she started singing.

We all yelled, "No! Please!" but it was too late. I had that dumb tune stuck in my head all day, and even all night. Dad said he heard me singing "So don't forget to wipe when you don't wear a diape-rrrrrrrr" in my sleep.

On Sunday, Dad had to go into work. He's a super in a big apartment building close to my school called the Monroe. His job is to fix stuff that breaks. Not stuff that belongs to people, like a teapot or a saxophone or someone's tooth. Stuff that belongs to the building, like heaters and doorbells and windows.

The elevator in the Monroe stopped working on Sunday, so Dad had to go check things out.

I begged him to let me come. Here's why: The Monroe has ten floors, with a whole bunch of apartments on each floor. I don't know multiplication yet, but what I do know is that adds up to tons of people, which adds up to tons of signatures.

Dad has worked in the Monroe ever since I can remember. So I have gone there a lot, and I have been banned from doing a lot of things there, including:

1. Pretending to be the elevator operator.

2. Doing headstands in the lobby.

3. Filming horror movies in the staircase.

4. Entering the gym. At all. Who knew ten-pound weights were so heavy? Who knew a running machine could go so fast?

Eyes on the Prize

But I was *not* banned from collecting signatures near the mailboxes.

While Dad was busy working on the elevator, I went into his little office and dragged out a tiny card table, which I put by the mailboxes. Then I dragged out a folding chair. I put the petition on the table, next to a sign that said:

HELP A KID!

TAKE A DOUGHNUT!

Then I put out the box of powdered mini doughnuts Dad had brought home the day before. He always says that powdered doughnuts are his kryptonite. He cannot resist their tempting tastiness. You can always tell when he's eaten one because the white powder gets on his brown mustache.

The Fix-It Friends

Maybe it was the doughnuts or maybe it was my charm, but either way, after just one hour, our petition had ninety-five signatures. I was starting to run low on doughnuts when Ezra and his mom, Principal Powell, passed by. They live in the Monroe, so I had been expecting them.

Ezra is Jude's best friend. Sometimes I tell people he is my best friend, too, but Jude gets angry and jealous and tells me to knock it off. He says that Ezra only hangs out with me because I'm Jude's little sister and he has to. But I know that's not true.

Ezra and I have lots in common. I love to sing, and Ezra loves to record music. He has been recording my demo album called *One Tough Cookie* on his computer. I already have two and a half songs finished. Sometimes Minnie plays the piano while I sing, but if she doesn't, it's okay because Ezra can make music on his computer.

Eyes on the Prize

He can make it sound like there's a whole band playing for me.

One day, when I'm older, I will walk down the red carpet and win a big music award, and Ezra is going to be the first person I thank in my acceptance speech. Do you know who I will not thank? People who always doubted me. People named Jude B. Conti.

You know what else Ezra and I have in common? Our love of powdered mini doughnuts.

I handed him and his mom doughnuts as I told them all about our 100 Days project and how I was dying to win the trophy.

"Veronica, this is a fantastic project," said Principal Powell as Ezra signed his name. "Whether or not you get a trophy, you've done excellent work. And that's really what matters, isn't it?"

She said it like she was warning me not to get my hopes up . . . which made me feel a little disappointed.

"Yeah, Ronny, trophies are overrated—trust me," said Ezra. He knows because he has a bunch of them, for his super-cool robotics creations. He should have a trophy for speed talking because he is the fastest talker I've ever heard in all my life. "Most of the time, the trophies you win are flimsy and they break. Especially if you have a crazy kitten that knocks them over when he runs back and forth on your shelves like a lunatic."

Just then something started beeping, and Ezra looked down at his watch. Ezra's watch looks like it could belong to James Bond. It glows in the dark and has a timer on it, and you can wear it underwater. Plus, it beeps!

"Ez," I said. "Your watch is trying to tell you something."

"Oh, it's just a reminder. I programmed it to remind me when I'm supposed to do something because otherwise I'd totally forget." Ezra cracked his knuckles. He has a habit of doing this, and I have told him and told him not to because Nana says it's bad for you, but he never listens.

"That beep is reminding me I have to finish my social studies project," he said. "So I'd better go."

They walked away, and I was admiring all the beautiful signatures on my petition when I heard a grumpy voice. It grumbled, "Young lady, you know perfectly well that loitering is not permitted by the mailboxes."

I didn't have to look up to know it was Mr. Luntzgarten, who lives on the fourth floor. He is the only person anywhere who calls me "young lady."

"I'm not littering!" I protested. "I don't even have any garbage."

"I didn't say *litter*ing," he replied with a scowl. When he scowls, his humongous gray eyebrows get scrunched together. It makes them look like one big eyebrow, which is even creepier than normal. "Loitering. Hanging around without an official purpose. Don't they teach vocabulary in school anymore?"

Eyes on the Prize

He leaned over my table and peered at the petition. I got a close-up look at the hat he always wears, which is brown and checkered and very old-fashioned. It's the kind of hat people wear in the black-and-white movies that Ezra likes.

All of a sudden, Mr. Luntzgarten stood up straight. His enormous eyebrows were not in their scrunched-up-and-mad position. Instead, they were raised up in their surprised-and-very-curious position.

"I see Miss Tibbs signed your list," he said.

I had totally forgotten that I introduced Miss Tibbs and Mr. Luntzgarten. We were at a party at Ezra's house, and they both got very excited about fruitcake, which is how I knew they would be a match made in heaven.

"Oh yes," I replied. "Miss Tibbs is a *big* fan of our petition."

Mr. Luntzgarten was quiet for a second, like he was thinking about something. Then he picked up the pen and signed his name. After his name, he wrote his phone number.

"Just in case you need to contact me . . . to, uh . . . to follow up." His cheeks got red. "I've signed many petitions. It's standard."

I was so grateful and surprised that Mr. Luntzgarten signed the petition. I grabbed the last mini doughnut in the box and jumped up to hand it to him. But when I jumped up, I accidentally knocked over the card table. The petition and pencils flew up in the air. So did the powdered doughnut box . . . and all the white powder at the bottom. It puffed up in the air like a big snow cloud and landed oh-so-gently all over Mr. Luntzgarten's black coat.

Eyes on the Prize

The bad news: Now there is a fifth thing I am banned from doing at the Monroe.

The good news: I had ninety-eight signatures on our petition!

Chapter 8

On Monday morning, I was so excited to show my 100 Days group that the petition was almost full. I did a little dance to the jazz music Miss Mabel was playing very softly from her desk.

"Ta-DA!" I cried. "Ninety-eight signatures!"

"How'd you get all those?" asked Minnie.

"I guess I just have a way with words." I grinned from ear to ear.

I turned to Matt. "So you only need to get two signatures. You can handle that, can't you?"

Matt rolled his hazel eyes.

"Yes, I *think* I can handle that," he said very sarcastically.

And I believed him. After all, anyone could have gotten two signatures. I could have gotten two signatures on a totally deserted island, for crying out loud!

But I was wrong.

The next day, on Tuesday, we got into our 100 Days groups—well, all of us except Minnie. She had to leave school early to get ready for her big recital. Miss Mabel walked over to our group and asked to see our project so far. That's when Matt told us there was a problem.

"Just a little one," he said.

But there is no such thing as a little problem when you're dealing with Matthew Sawyer.

"You didn't get the signatures! I knew it!" I exclaimed.

"Of *course* I got the signatures!" Matt replied. "The petition is all done! The problem is . . . well, I, uh . . ." He started rubbing the back of his head.

"Oh no!" I cried. "You forgot it at home!"

Matt stared down at the floor, but this time, it wasn't because he was looking for water bugs. It was because he was about to cry. I could tell because his face was red and his eyes were all wet. I had never seen Matthew Sawyer cry before, and even though he was my enemy, I felt really bad for him.

"It's okay, Matt," said Miss Mabel. She put her hand on his shoulder.

"I'm really sorry," he said to her, with a quivery voice. "I don't know how I forgot it this morning. I was reading this really good book about parasites, and I was so into it, I guess the project just slipped my mind."

Eyes on the Prize

"It's all right!" chirped Cora. "Everyone makes mistakes!"

"Yeah, but I make mistakes all the time," Matt said. His voice was so soft I could hardly hear him. "I don't mean to. My mom says I just get distracted."

I was surprised to see Matt look so miserable. I had no idea he felt so bad when he forgot stuff.

He always made jokes, which made me think he didn't care. I felt sorry for giving him a hard time about his mistakes, and I just really wanted to make him feel better.

"Are you using that checklist I made for you? To help you remember what to bring from home?" asked Miss Mabel.

"I *would* use it," he said, sniffing, "except I can't find it."

"Well, I think you need a new checklist," she said. "Is there someone who can help you make another one?"

Matt wiped his eyes with the back of his hand. He shrugged.

That's when I got a huge brain wave! I gasped loudly. Gasping is a specialty of mine.

"I know someone who can help!" I cried. "My brother, Jude! He writes lists in his sleep. Seriously. He has dreams of the lists he wants to make."

"Is he the fourth grader that keeps reorganizing the Lost and Found box?" Miss Mabel asked.

I nodded.

"He does seem like the perfect guy for the job," she said.

Matt did not look so convinced, but Miss Mabel told him that his homework that night was to make a good, solid checklist with Jude. So he had no choice.

"This is perfect!" I said after Miss Mabel left. "Ezra is coming over after school, and Cora, too. So we can have a whole Fix-It Friends meeting to help you."

I thought Matt would be very happy and oh-so-thankful. He was not.

"I'm not broken." Matt scowled. "I don't need to be fixed."

"We don't fix *people*!" said Cora. "Just problems that people have."

"Like how you get distracted and forget stuff," I said.

"You're right," he said. "I have a *huge* forgetting problem. So I wouldn't be surprised if I forgot to come to your house after school."

I sighed really loudly. Matt was already back to driving me bonkers.

"If you let the Fix-Its help you, I promise that I will never stomp on a water bug again."

"Never?" he asked.

"Well, at least not for the rest of second grade."

He thought about it for a second.

"And do you promise never to tell that offensive joke again?" he asked.

"Oh, for crying out loud!" I exclaimed. "It's not offensive!"

"What joke is it?" asked Cora.

"What lies dead on its back, one hundred feet up in the air?" I asked.

"I give up," said Cora.

"A centipede!"

Cora and I giggled, but Matt crossed his arms and glowered at us.

"It's offensive to centipedes," he said.

"Okay, okay," I said. "I'll stop telling the joke. So will you come over?"

"Fine," he grumbled. "But I hope your brother is not as annoying as you."

That made me laugh so hard, I couldn't breathe.

"Oh, just you wait," I told him.

Chapter 9

As soon as we got to my house after school, I made a hot and tasty winter drink for everyone. It's called a Bop Shoo Bop. Here's how you make it:

1. Put a cup of milk in the microwave for 45 seconds.
2. Add a packet of instant hot chocolate.
3. Add in three shakes of cinnamon.
4. Plop on five mini marshmallows.
5. Stick a cherry on top.

There's only one thing better than a cherry on top, and that's two cherries on top.

Eyes on the Prize

Pearl sat right next to Matt at our kitchen table. She is oh-so-curious about people she has never met before. She stared at him as she hugged Ricardo and sipped her drink. Then, suddenly, she pulled on the sleeve of Matt's striped shirt and said, "I'm so big! I go potty! I go AWW the time!"

I thought he'd snicker or say something dumb. But to my surprise, he turned to her with a big, bright smile and exclaimed, "You do? Wow! That's so cool! You really are big!"

Then he asked her what her rat's name was, and she said, "Wicawdo. He's fwiendly."

"Yeah, rats get a bad rap, but they are usually really friendly," he said. "You know, they get blamed for starting the bubonic plague. But it wasn't the rats that did it. You know who did it?"

Pearl was looking at him with wide eyes. "Who?"

"Gerbils!" he said. "So they're the bad ones. Not rats!"

"Bad gewbiws!" she said, making her mad face.

I gave Cora a look that said, *Can you believe this?* Because never in a million years would I have guessed that Matthew Sawyer would be so nice to my baby sister!

When we'd gulped down every drop of our Bop Shoo Bops, Cora, Matt, and I went to find Jude and Ezra.

They were hunched over Jude's neat and tidy desk. Their foreheads were wrinkled like they were concentrating hard.

"Ninety-three, ninety-four," Jude counted.

"Hey there!" I exclaimed. "What's cooking?"

Jude groaned. "You messed up our count!" he hollered. "Now we have to start all over again!"

"It's okay," said Ezra. "I think we messed up that count, anyway."

I wished for the ten thousandth time that Ezra could live with us instead of Jude. He never yells at me for being a slob, and he laughs at all my jokes. He also has an adorable kitten. He would be the perfect roommate.

"What are you doing for your 100 Days project?" I asked Ezra.

"We're writing a story with one hundred sentences," Ezra said speedily. "And for the illustration, we are making a drawing with exactly one hundred pencil strokes."

"That is very cool," I said, "but I think you might want to add a tad more razzle-dazzle."

"Razzle-dazzle?" Jude snorted. "You don't need razzle-dazzle when you have a great idea."

"Hey, you know, a little bling might not be the worst idea," said Ezra. "Just to jazz up the presentation."

"Yeah," I agreed. "Just to jazz it up. Give it pizzazz."

I love words with *z*'s in them, and words with double *z*'s are even better.

"We don't need jazz or pizzazz, and we definitely don't need razzle-dazzle," Jude said.

"Suit yourself." I shrugged. "Listen, we need to have a Fix-It Friends meeting, for Matt."

"Maybe later," said Jude, looking down at his project. "We're in the middle of something."

Eyes on the Prize

"Not later," I insisted. "It has to be ASAP! Pronto! Without delay! Matt's here just for that reason, and plus Miss Mabel told us to."

"You can't just order everyone around all the time," grumbled Jude. "You're not the boss of the world."

"That's what I tell her!" said Matt.

"So buzz off," Jude said, and he waved me away, like a mosquito.

Then Cora said the magic word. "We need to make a list!" she said quickly. "Can you help us?"

That got his attention, all right. He looked up at us and started to laugh.

"Can I help you make a list?" he asked. "Can a bird fly? Can a dolphin swim?"

He put his pencil down and leaned back in his chair. "Tell me everything."

Chapter 10

We told Jude all about how sometimes Matt had trouble paying attention, which meant he sometimes forgot stuff, which meant our 100 Days project was in danger! Jude nodded slowly.

"I'm going to let you in on a little secret," said Jude. "I know I'm famous around town for never forgetting anything. I know people think that I'm Mr. Perfect—"

"Don't forget Mr. Big Head," I added. Matt started to chuckle, but Jude gave him a dirty look, and he clammed up.

"But the truth is," Jude continued, "I forget stuff all the time. There's only one thing I never forget. You know what that is?"

"To pat yourself on the back?" I asked. Matt covered his mouth to squash his laugh.

"The one thing I never forget"—Jude paused to make sure we were really listening—"is to check my lists."

"Cool," said Matt.

"Oh, it is *more* than cool," corrected Jude. "It's the key to staying organized! And staying organized is the key to success!! So it's the key to success!"

"Ummm, okay," said Matt. I could tell he was regretting coming over. And he thought *I* was annoying! Ha!

Jude insisted that Matt needed five different lists, but Ezra talked him down to two, which Ezra typed up on his laptop. When Jude gets excited, Ezra is the one person who can talk reason to him.

We made a morning checklist for Matt to keep at home:

MORNING CHECKLIST

1. Homework in folder?
2. Folder in backpack?
3. Lunch box?
4. Special projects?

We also made an afternoon checklist, for Matt to check before he left school:

AFTERNOON CHECKLIST

1. Books for homework?
2. Homework folder?

3. Lunch box?

4. Sneakers?

Matt said he didn't need to put sneakers on the list, but then I reminded him about how on pajama day, he left his sneakers in the classroom and walked out the door with bare feet.

Dad came in to see what we were doing. When he heard about the lists, he said, "I'm terrible at remembering stuff. You know what I do? I put a Post-it on my desk or the fridge. A big, bright one that I can't ignore. Then I write 'Bring chain saw' or whatever on it."

Matt gulped loudly. "You really have a chain saw?"

"Oh, I've got loads of 'em," said Dad. I gave Matt my best *Told you so!* look.

Just then we heard a loud jingly sound coming from the bathroom.

Jude, Dad, and I looked at one another.

"Oh no!" we all moaned at the same exact time.

Monster Potty played:

When you really have to go,

Here's what you need to know—

"Have mercy, Father!" I wailed. I always call my dad *Dad*, but when I'm trying to be dramatic, I call him *Father*.

Eyes on the Prize

"The potty of doom must go!" declared Jude.

So don't forget to wipe

When you don't wear a diape-

Rrrrrrrrrrr!

"Awwww," said Cora. "I think the song's kind of cute."

"Just you wait," I told her. "The potty song strikes in your brain when you least expect it."

"Yeah, tonight you'll be lying peacefully in bed, counting sheep," said Jude, "when suddenly these words will ring in your ears—"

"It's potty time! It's potty time! It's potty time! It's potty time!" We both sang along with the potty, at the top of our lungs.

Chapter 11

A few minutes later, the doorbell rang, so I ran downstairs to answer it.

I absolutely love answering the door. It could be anyone! It could be a record producer who heard me singing out my window and wants to make me a star! It could be a stray Great Dane who needs a home and just happened to press my doorbell with his nose.

Nana is always telling me, "Be-a care-a-ful! Neva open da door-a to-a stranger-a!" Which is why I always look through the glass window in the door to see who it is before I open it.

Eyes on the Prize

The person I saw through the glass was not a record producer or a Great Dane.

It was a girl I'd never met before. Here's what she looked like:

1. Straight black hair pulled back into a neat ponytail.

2. Tortoiseshell eyeglasses, just like Jude's.

3. An enormous backpack on her back. The backpack was so big, she was hunched over. She looked like a turtle with a huge shell on her back.

4. The biggest book ever in her arms.

"Who are *you*?" I asked. I had to talk kind of loud so she could hear through the glass.

"I'm Chloe," she said. "Matt's sister. I came to pick him up."

I was dumbstruck. No, that does not mean I was turned into a dumbbell, which is what I used to think. It means I turned speechless.

"Matthew Sawyer has a sister?" I asked.

"Yep," she said. "And she is me. I mean, I'm her."

"But you don't even look like him!" I said.

She smiled. "That's because we're stepsiblings. His mom and my dad got married a few years ago."

Eyes on the Prize

I shouted up to Matt: "DO YOU HAVE A SISTER NAMED CHLOE WHO WEARS AN ENORMOUS BACKPACK WHO IS PICKING YOU UP TODAY?"

Like my grandma says, "You-a neva can-a be too-a careful!"

"YES!" he shouted back.

So I let her in.

I was full of questions. I asked Chloe how old she was (thirteen) and did she live with Matt (half of the week) and what the heck was that gigantic book she was holding.

"Oh, it's the dictionary," she said. "I'm trying to read the whole thing."

She sat down at the kitchen table as I made her a Bop Shoo Bop.

Jude came into the kitchen to get a glass of water. When he saw Chloe and her dictionary, he got excited.

"Oh, cool! I've always wanted to read the dictionary!" he exclaimed. "What letter are you up to?"

"I'm only up to *c*." She sighed. "There are so many *c* words!"

"There *are* so many *c* words!" Jude agreed. He nodded so hard, his glasses slid down his nose and he had to push them back up. "Even just the words that start with *con*!"

"*Contain, contend, conversation,*" Chloe said.

"*Control, conference, concentrate,*" Jude added.

"Our last name!" I burst out. "Conti!"

Jude said, "Don't you have to help Matt finish his lists?"

Then he turned back to Chloe. "*Connive.*"

"*Contract!*" she laughed.

"*Congress!*" he laughed.

Eyes on the Prize

I had never heard Jude have so much fun with anyone besides Ezra. It was like they were two people sharing one big brain.

I went back upstairs, where Ezra was printing out the lists for Matt.

"Matt," I said. "Your sister is really smart."

"Yeah, so I heard," he replied. "She can be a total show-off."

"I know how you feel," I said.

Pearl ran in then, holding Ricardo. She scrambled up onto Matt's lap and asked him to tell her a story about the bad gerbils.

And he did. He made up a story about a gerbil named Jerry who started the bubonic plague and a good little rat named Reginald who was framed for the whole thing.

"Reginald died many, many years ago," he said,

"but his great-great-great-great-great-great-great-great-great-great-grandson is still alive. And do you know what his name is?"

She shook her head. She was so mesmerized by Matt's story that her mouth was hanging open.

"Ricardo!" he said.

She made a yelp of surprise. Then, to my amazement, she threw her arms around Matt and said, "My best fwiend!"

Eyes on the Prize

And to my even greater amazement, he hugged her back.

My sister was best friends with Matthew Sawyer.

My brother was best friends with Matthew Sawyer's sister.

Life is full of surprises.

Chapter 12

The checklist worked! At least, I think it did, because Matt remembered to bring in the petition the next morning. It also could have been the fact that I called him five times before school.

The first time I said, "Rise and shine! Remember to bring the petition!"

The second time, I said, "Did you put it in your backpack?"

The third time: "Are you sure?"

The fourth: "Super, super sure?"

And then: "You didn't take it out again, did you? Can I talk to Chloe just to make sure?"

Eyes on the Prize

When we showed Miss Mabel the petition, she was so impressed and so flattered.

"You guys are the best," she said. "I'm really proud of you."

When Miss Mabel is proud of you, it feels spectacular. It feels like drinking an ice-cold lemonade on a hot day, with a bulldog puppy licking your face and your favorite song playing on the radio.

Since we were done with the petition, we could move on to the last step of our project—decorating our poster.

That day during math, we drew a big number *100* in the middle of the poster, and Minnie decorated the space around it with one hundred musical notes. Then, after school, the whole group came over to my house to finish the poster. Even Minnie came, because she finally had a little break from piano lessons.

"So how'd the recital go?" I asked. "Were you allegro when you played allegro?"

"Yep!" she said. "And afterward, I got a trophy!"

"It's raining trophies all around me!" I moaned. "But I'm stuck under an umbrella!"

As soon as we had gotten home, our group started working on the poster in the living room.

"Sequins time!" Cora yelled.

She took out a bag filled with about five billion red sequins. They were left over from the

Eyes on the Prize

Queen of Hearts costume she'd made for our school play.

"You sure you won't go overboard?" Minnie asked with her eyebrows raised.

Cora nodded.

"You should take an oath," I said, raising my right hand in the air. "Repeat after me: I, Cora Klein, do solemnly swear . . ."

Cora repeated my words.

". . . to control myself when gluing sequins on things."

Minnie piped up. "I shall never glue sequins on a musical instrument or on human hair."

Cora repeated everything.

"Now say, 'Cross my heart and hope to cry and never eat a whoopie pie,'" I said.

She did promise. So I handed over the glue.

"We'll get snacks," I told Cora. "Remember your oath."

Minnie and I went into the kitchen. We found Matt and Pearl in there, eating ants on a log. It's Matt's favorite snack. Of course.

Matt was saying to Pearl, "So when a water bug crosses your path, what do you do?"

"Weave it awone!" she replied.

"That's right!" he said, patting her head. "Want a raisin?"

Pearl popped some raisins in her mouth. Then she ran out to find Ricardo so he could have a taste.

Minnie, Matt, and I made nachos. There weren't any of my favorite nacho toppings in the fridge, so we had to improvise. We melted mozzarella on top and dripped tomato sauce over that.

"Pizza nachos!" I exclaimed.

Eyes on the Prize

"Hmmmn," said Minnie, taking a little taste. "They're kind of gross but also kind of delicious."

Matt shoved a whole nacho into his mouth and said with his mouth full, "Ahhh, my favorite—grossalicious!"

Suddenly, we heard Pearl shouting from the living room. We ran in to investigate.

"WICAWDO!" she hollered. "He's WUINED!"

I looked on the table, next to our 100 Days poster. There was Ricardo, only he looked different. Lots of little red sequins glittered all over his dirty black fur. He looked like he had a fancy case of the chicken pox.

"Cora!" I scolded. "You promised!"

Cora's face was as red as the sequins.

"I'm so sorry," she said. "I guess I do get carried away."

I looked at Ricardo, with his too-big bunny panties and his tail duct-taped on and now the sequins all over his body. I shook my head.

"Ricardo had no dignity left," I said sadly. "And now he has less than none."

Pearl made her most furious face at Cora.

"You bad—wike the gewbiws," she said, wagging her finger.

Then she grabbed Ricardo and stormed out.

I zipped the bag of sequins closed.

"I still love you, and you're still my best friend forever and ever and ever," I told her. "But I am taking these away! For your own good."

"At least the poster looks good," Cora said.

Eyes on the Prize

It did look good.

It looked good, but not great. It needed a finishing touch.

Minnie munched on a pizza nacho. "It needs a border."

"What about silver gum wrappers?" Matt said. "I have a hundred of them from the 100 Days project I did last year."

"Oh yeah, that's right," I said. "Didn't your group bring in a humongous gum wad, made from chewing one hundred pieces of gum?"

"Yeah, and I *still* don't see why we didn't win," he grumbled.

The silver wrappers did seem like they'd be the perfect finishing touch. So when Matt went home, I handed him our poster with the petition attached.

Chapter 13

After everyone left, we had minestrone for dinner. That's just Italian for vegetable soup.

I am not a big fan of most vegetables, but I am a big fan of vegetable soup. It is one of the great mysteries of the world. Of course, to make the minestrone good, you have to put a big pile of Parmesan on it. That's the secret ingredient.

I had just had my first spoonful of minestrone when the phone rang. Even though Mom and Dad don't like it when we answer the phone during dinner, I could not resist. A ringing phone makes me so curious.

Eyes on the Prize

Jude always says, "Curiosity killed the cat!"

And I say, "Well, cats have nine lives."

And Jude says, "Well, it probably killed him all nine times."

And Mom always says, "Are you really arguing about this? Really?"

I love answering the phone because absolutely anyone could be on the other end. Once, I answered the phone and a voice said, "Congratulations! You have won forty thousand dollars!" I almost fainted with excitement. But when I gave Mom the phone, she said it was a scam.

When I answered the phone that night, it wasn't a person telling me I'd won a sweepstakes or anything fun like that. It was Matthew Sawyer.

"What's wrong?" I asked right away.

"Why do you think something's wrong?" he asked. "Maybe I'm just calling you to tell you everything is perfect and we are all ready for tomorrow."

"*Are* you calling me to tell me that everything is perfect and we are all ready for tomorrow?"

"No," he said. "Something's wrong."

"MATTHEW SAWYER!" I shouted at the top of my lungs. "WHAT HAPPENED?"

"Do you want the good news or bad news first?"

"Good news," I said right away. I always want the good news first.

"The good news is that there were plenty of gum wrappers, and the other good news is that I glued every single one on, and the best news is that it looked really, really, really great."

"So what's the bad news?"

"After I did all that, I lost the project."

Eyes on the Prize

I was so furious, I stomped my foot down. I stomped it so hard, I thought my foot might go right through the floor.

"This is SERIOUS!" I told Matt. "We need that project first thing tomorrow morning or we're toast! And not the good kind of toast, with heaps of butter and strawberry jam on it. We're burned toast. *Capisce?*"

"I know," said Matt softly. "I can't believe I lost it. I bet you think I'm the worst."

I *had* sort of been thinking that, but as soon as I heard his voice get so sad, I stopped being furious at him.

"I don't think you're the worst," I said. "And anyway, you're in luck. I just so happen

to be the president of a world-famous group of problem solvers. I can fix this in a jiff. Be right over!"

Then I hung up the phone and raced into the living room shouting, "Code red! Code red! Code red!"

"It's happened," Jude said. "She's lost her last marble."

Pearl stood up in her high chair, waving her arms and shouting, "CODE WED! CODE WED!" Which would have made me laugh if I wasn't totally freaking out.

Mom said she'd take me to Matt's house as soon as we finished dinner, so I sloshed big spoonfuls of soup into my mouth as fast as I could.

Jude insisted on coming, too. I knew it was just because he wanted to talk to Chloe, but I didn't care. We needed all the help we could get.

Chapter 14

Dr. Sawyer answered the door. She has the same hazel eyes as Matt and the same brown hair, only hers is long and shiny. She must have just come home from working at the hospital because she was still in her blue doctor uniform that looks just like pajamas. That's one reason I'd love to be a doctor. You get to wear pajamas to work.

There was a smudge of red on her top. When I saw it, I gulped hard.

"Um, Dr. Sawyer?" I said. "You have a little blood on your shirt."

She looked down, stuck her finger in the smudge, and popped her finger in her mouth. Then she laughed.

"It's ketchup," she said. "I was just eating a burger and fries."

Then Dr. Sawyer invited Mom into the kitchen for a cup of tea, and she told Jude and me that we could go upstairs.

We got to the top of the stairs and saw a beautiful blue bedroom with clouds painted on the wall near the ceiling. There was a tidy bed, piled high with fluffy pillows. In the corner, there was a desk full of books, and sitting at the desk was Chloe, hunched over her dictionary.

"Hi there," she said.

"What letter are you up to now?" asked Jude.

"*I*," she said. "And if you think there are a lot of *con* words, just wait until you get to the *in* words!"

Eyes on the Prize

"*Inform, inquire, intelligence,*" Jude rattled off.

"*Involve, insist, interfere,*" Chloe added.

"In need of help!" I cried. "Which is what we are! Because of your brother! Where is his room, anyway?"

"The next door over," said Chloe. "Enter at your own risk."

I walked down the hall, but Jude stayed behind with Chloe, thinking up more *in* words. I was wondering what Chloe had meant by "enter at your own risk." Then I got to Matt's doorway, and I knew.

Matthew Sawyer's room was an enormous, gigantic, *ginormous* mess.

On every single inch of the room were heaps of books and Lego pieces and candy wrappers and empty cups and shoes and trading cards and comics and soccer balls and lots and lots of striped shirts. You couldn't even see the floor or the furniture.

His bed and desk and dresser just looked like big mountains of stuff.

It took me a minute to even find Matt in the middle of it all. But finally, I spotted him, lying on his stomach on the floor, reading a book about spiders.

"Matthew Sawyer!" I cried.

"Oh, hey, what's up?" he asked oh-so-casually.

Eyes on the Prize

He said it like there was nothing at all the matter. "Did Pearl come with you? I read an article about the plague I wanted to tell her about."

I was speechless. Truly speechless! I opened my mouth, but no sound came out.

I just started pacing back and forth. Or, at least, I tried to pace. His floor was so messy, I couldn't even walk! I just kept tripping!

"Matthew Sawyer!" I exclaimed. "Your room—it's—it's—"

My mom always says that if I don't have anything nice to say, I shouldn't say anything at all. So I was trying to think of a nice way to say "disaster."

But he finished my sentence: "It's cool, I know. Did you see my mealworm? It's in the larvae stage."

"Your room is a hideous nightmare!" I screeched. "No wonder you can't find our project! You probably can't even find your bed!"

"Sure I can." He walked over to a big lump and said, "Here it is!"

But then he patted it a bit and said, "Strike that. This is my desk. But don't worry. I know my bed is in here somewhere. And so is our project."

"We're doomed," I moaned. "We're sunk. We're the *Titanic*."

Eyes on the Prize

I sank down to the ground, but instead of my butt hitting the floor, it hit something very gooey and sticky. I stood up and looked at my backside. It was covered in a bright green gloop.

Matt smiled. "Oh good! You found my oobleck!"

"JUDE!" I shouted. "CHLOE! ANYONE!"

Chapter 15

Jude's face went pale when he saw Matt's room.

"You've been robbed!" he cried. "Call the police!"

"No, no, there were no robbers," said Chloe.

"I don't understand," said Jude. "If there was an earthquake, why would it only hit Matt's room and not the rest of the house?"

Chloe laughed. "Because there was no earthquake. This is just what Matt's room looks like."

"But—but—but . . ."

Jude was stuttering like a robot who was short-circuiting.

Eyes on the Prize

I snapped my fingers in front of his face to wake him out of his shock.

"Jude!" I exclaimed. "Pull yourself together! Underneath this mess somewhere is our trophy-winning project. You have to help us find it!"

"I can't believe I'm saying this," said Jude. "But I don't think we can do it."

I put my hands on his shoulders and looked right in his eyes. "Listen to me! You are Jude B—"

His eyes got wide and panicky because he thought I was going to say his middle name, right there in front of Chloe. But I have vowed I'd never tell anyone what his middle name is, and I never would.

"You're Jude B. Conti!" I exclaimed. "This is your destiny. You were born to battle this Monster Mess. Now take a deep breath and tell us what to do first."

Jude didn't do anything for a moment. Then he nodded very fast and said, "Chloe, you're on clothing. Fold clothing and place it in drawers."

He turned to me. "Ronny, you're on books, magazines, any kind of papers—sort into piles."

I hate it when he calls me Ronny, but I bit my tongue this once.

Then he turned to Matt, who was still reading his spider book on the floor. He slammed the book

closed and barked, "Matt, you're in charge of"—he picked up the bowl of oobleck with a grimace—"gross, unexplained goo stuff."

"What are *you* in charge of?" I asked.

"I am in charge of everything," Jude said, looking like the King of the World.

At first, it felt like we weren't even making a dent. Slowly but surely, though, we cleared off enough stuff so that the furniture appeared.

"My motto is: a place for everything and everything in its place," Jude lectured as we worked.

"He is not exaggerating," I said. "He has a pillow with those exact words embroidered on it."

While we sorted the stuff, Jude found a bunch of empty plastic containers, some paper, and tape. That was all he needed to go label-crazy.

He labeled one box MAGNIFYING GLASSES and another box SCIENCE EXPERIMENT SUPPLIES. There was a COMIC BOOK box and a MODELING MATERIALS box and about a dozen others. He even labeled one box LABELING SUPPLIES.

While we were cleaning, we found a lot of stuff:

1. Eight homework packets.

2. Six library books.

3. Three missing puzzle pieces.

4. A roll of Christmas wrapping paper.

5. A bag of potatoes. All the potatoes had grown eyes. They had eyes so big, they could practically wear mascara!

But did we find the project?

No, we did not.

Just as we were about to give up, Dr. Sawyer stuck her head in the door.

"What does your poster look like?" she asked.

Eyes on the Prize

"It's got a hundred red sequins in the middle and a hundred musical notes around that and a hundred gum wrappers on the sides," I said.

"Does it look something like this?" she asked. Then she stepped into the room holding our poster!

"Yes!" Matt exclaimed. "Where the heck did you find it?"

"In the laundry room, on top of the dryer," she said.

"Oh yeahhhhhhhhh," he said, nodding. "I put it there to dry."

I wanted to clobber him. I wanted to pummel him. I wanted to give him a knuckle sandwich.

But his mother and his sister were standing right there, and besides, I knew he hadn't done it on purpose. So I just said, "Thanks, Dr. Sawyer," and took the poster out of her hands.

We got home so late that I didn't even change into my pj's. I just dropped into bed and fell asleep in about two minutes.

But before I drifted off, I said to Jude in the top bunk, "Hey, Jude?"

"No singing," he muttered sleepily.

"I'm not singing," I said. "I'm talking to you."

"Uh-huh?" he murmured.

"Thanks," I said. "I couldn't have done it without you."

But all I heard from the top bunk was snoring. He was already asleep.

Chapter 16

The next morning was the hundredth day of school! Miss Mabel was dressed for the occasion. She was wearing a headband that had a big silver number *100 boing*-ing around on top of springs.

"My oh my, Miss Mabel, you're magnificent!" I said.

"Right back at you," she said to me. "You're rocking the red today."

"Thank you!" I said, spinning around in my homemade red dress. "It's from my aunt Alice. She knows how to sew. Guess what I'm going to ask her to make me for my birthday next month."

"A leotard for when you win the Olympics?" asked Miss Mabel.

"Good idea . . . but no," I said. "I'm going to ask for a sari."

Miss Mabel put her arm around my shoulders and gave a big squeeze.

Cora and Minnie were both dressed up, too. Cora was in a yellow dress that was pleated and poufy with a patent leather belt. Minnie was wearing her piano recital outfit of black velvet pants and a silky white shirt. She was chewing on the ends of her braids.

"*¡Comer cabello humano es malo para la digestión!*" I said, pretending to be stern.

"*¡Por eso es que tengo un dolor de estómago!*" she replied.

"What's that mean?" I asked.

Eyes on the Prize

"So *that's* why I have a stomachache!" she said, and we both cracked up.

The morning seemed to stretch on forever, but finally it was time to go to the second-grade 100 Days gallery.

There were so many cool projects! As my dad would say, we had some stiff competition. These were the best ones:

1. A gigantic chocolate-chip cookie with one hundred chocolate chips in it.

2. A paper-doll chain with one hundred paper dolls.

3. A little schoolhouse made from one hundred Popsicle sticks.

The one I was most worried about was a beautiful green parrot made from one hundred feathers stuck in Styrofoam. It was so pretty and realistic, and I thought it would win for sure.

But then I walked past where our project was displayed, and I saw a big crowd of kids standing in front of it.

"There's my name!" one girl squealed.

"Do you see mine?" asked a boy.

"Oh, look! My sister signed, too, and Mrs. Rose! Cool!"

I turned to Cora and whispered, "They love our project!"

I noticed that Miss Tibbs was taking a long

time looking at our project. Then I saw her scribbling something on a piece of paper and slipping it into the pocket of her black pants.

I couldn't get close enough to see, but I knew it must be Mr. Luntzgarten's phone number that she'd written down. I could practically hear the wedding bells ringing! I could practically feel the petals I would toss as the flower girl!

When everyone had a chance to see the projects, Miss Mabel handed out ballots.

Then we all went into the auditorium to watch a video about a second-grade class in China that also did a 100 Days project. I knew Miss Mabel and the other teachers were counting up all the votes, so I was really nervous. It didn't just feel like there were butterflies in my stomach. It felt like there was a bunch of super-excited Chihuahuas in there.

When the video was over, Principal Powell walked onto the stage and said, "Well, ladies and gentlemen, the results are in! First, I just wanted to say how impressed I am by all the projects. They are so unique. . . ."

She said a bunch more stuff, but I stopped listening because the Chihuahuas in my stomach were wrestling with one another, and I couldn't concentrate.

"This year's winner of the second-grade 100 Days Contest is . . ." She unfolded the piece of paper that had the winner written on it. I thought the Chihuahuas were going to jump right out of my mouth. The palms of my hands were so sweaty!

"From Miss Mabel's class . . . 100 Signatures Speak Up."

I grabbed Cora's and Minnie's hands and squeezed hard. Matt yelled, "Yes! Yes! Yes!" Then

Eyes on the Prize

Miss Mabel was saying, "Guys! Go up on the stage! She's calling your names!"

I walked down the aisle and up the stairs to the stage in a daze. I was so happy, I felt like I was floating on a whipped-cream cloud.

When we got to the stage, Principal Powell shook hands with each of us. Then Mrs. Rose handed each of us a big, heavy box. I did not know trophies came in boxes! I had so much to learn.

I lifted the top off the box, expecting to see the gleam of gold. I did see a gleam, but it was of red, and yellow, and blue, and green. Inside the box was a gum-ball machine.

"In recognition of your excellence," Principal Powell was saying, "we'd like to award each of you a gum-ball machine with exactly one hundred gum balls inside. Just don't eat them all at once. Your dentist will be *furious* at me."

Cora laughed. Minnie laughed. Matthew Sawyer laughed.

I did not laugh. I was too busy waiting for the part where I would get my trophy.

Then, before I knew what was happening, the principal was dismissing everyone and the rest of my group was walking offstage. As quick as a flash, I tugged on Principal Powell's sleeve and said, "Thank you very much for the gum balls. But when do we get the trophies?"

Principal Powell smiled brightly, which made me think her answer was going to be "Right now!"

Eyes on the Prize

But instead her answer was "Oh, we don't have trophies this year. We thought the gum balls were a bit more fun."

I knew I shouldn't feel disappointed, because I had just won and everyone clapped and I got a hundred gum balls and everything. But I did feel disappointed. I couldn't help it.

I didn't want Principal Powell to think I was ungrateful, so I nodded and glued a fake smile on my face. As Dad always says, "You gotta fake it till you make it."

Chapter 17

It was the end of the day, so when we got back to our classroom, Miss Mabel told us to pack up.

Everyone was congratulating me and asking for gum balls.

"Sure," I said. I handed out gum balls to anyone who asked.

I popped a red one in my mouth, then a yellow, then a blue, then another red, and the big burst of fruity flavor started to cheer me up.

I was just putting the top on my gum-ball machine box when Matt walked up to my desk. He handed me a big, lumpy envelope.

Eyes on the Prize

"Does this have one hundred boogers in it?" I asked. "Because I'm really not in the mood."

"No," he replied. "I could only collect nine, so I gave up."

"Is there a stink bomb in here?"

Matt shook his head.

"Worms?"

"Just open it, will you?" He sighed.

I was pretty suspicious, but I was also pretty curious. After a few seconds, my curiosity was stronger. So I tore open the envelope. Something heavy and shiny fell out onto my desk with a clatter.

It was a medal!

A shiny, golden medal with a big ribbon attached, with one blue stripe, one red stripe, and one white stripe. It looked just like what people who win at the Olympics get. The golden part had a big star in the middle, and it said, YOU'RE A STAR!

"Is this for me?" I asked.

Matt nodded.

"But..." I was so confused, I didn't even know what to say. "Why?"

Matt shrugged. "To say thanks or whatever."

Matt looked serious. He sounded serious. But it seemed impossible that he could be so... well, nice.

"Wait a *minute!*" I yelped. "Is it opposite day?"

Matt rolled his eyes. "No."

"Which means yes!"

"Whatever you say."

"What's the opposite of that?" I said. "Whatever I don't say? I don't get it."

"IT'S NOT OPPOSITE DAY!" he hollered.

Eyes on the Prize

"Okay, okay, you don't have to get so upset," I said.

Matt let out a huge sigh. "Do you want the medal or not?"

"What a ridiculous thing to ask! Of course I want it! I've been longing for a medal for my entire life."

I put the medal around my neck. It felt heavy, just like I thought it would.

"Thank you, Matthew Sawyer," I said. "I'm sorry I said your room was a hideous nightmare."

"It's okay," he said. "I'm sorry I put oobleck in your lunch box."

"It's okay." I replied. And then I said, "What? You did WHAT?"

But he was already running out the door of the classroom.

Chapter 18

At pickup, Dad let out a huge whoop when he saw me holding the gum-ball machine.

"Winner, winner, chicken dinner!" he shouted. I had no idea what that meant, but he sounded happy and proud.

"Wonny won?" asked Pearl from her stroller.

"Yes, Pearly Pie," I said. "Wonny won."

Jude walked over with a glum look on his face and nothing in his hands.

"Well, you win some, you lose some," Dad said, patting him on the back.

Eyes on the Prize

"I just don't get it," he said, shaking his head. "Our project was so complicated, and so perfect. And you know whose project won? Gary Grotowski's group! It was a top hat with a lever on it, and when you pulled the lever, one hundred pieces of confetti burst out."

"Sometimes the crowd just wants a little razzle-dazzle," said Dad, shrugging. "Whatcha gonna do?"

I had to bite on my tongue to keep myself from shouting, "Told you so! Told you so! Told you told you told you so!!"

I have done that to Jude before, and it only got me in trouble. Plus I felt sorry for the guy. He looked like a plant that hadn't been watered in a few days and was all wilted.

I offered him a gum ball, but he shook his head. And then who should I spot but Chloe, picking

Matt up. She was giving him a high five, which wasn't very easy for her to do, because she was carrying her enormous backpack and humongous dictionary.

I waved at her, and she and Matt walked over.

"You did it! Congrats!" she said.

Jude was suddenly looking much more cheerful. He was like a plant who had just gotten a big drink of fresh water. "Hey, *congratulations* is another *con* word."

"Yes!" Chloe laughed. "So is *confection*. And speaking of confections, I'm going to take Matt out for a treat, to celebrate. I hear the bakery across the street has delicious German chocolate cupcakes."

"I love German chocolate cake," I told her. "Mostly because when I was little, I used to think it was called German shepherd cake, and German shepherds are my fifth-favorite dog breed."

Eyes on the Prize

Chloe laughed. "You should all come!"

Jude turned to Dad. "Can we?"

"Why not?" Dad said. "Wasn't it Marie Antoinette who said, 'Let 'em eat cake'? That lady knew what she was talking about."

Then, at the same exact time, Jude and Chloe both said, "Actually, Marie Antoinette didn't say that."

"Yeah, she really said, 'Let them eat brioche,'" said Jude.

"Actually, I was reading a book about the French Revolution . . ." said Chloe, and the two of them walked together and talked about stuff that seemed pretty boring to me.

"I wanna vaniwa cake!" said Pearl. "I don't wike gewbiws. Or gewbiw chocowate."

"It's *German* chocolate, silly," I told her. "Not gerbil chocolate."

The Fix-It Friends

"Oh, hey, Pearl!" Matt said. "You just reminded me. I wanted to tell you about this article I read about gerbils. . . ."

Chloe and Jude were chatting behind me, and Matt and Pearl were chatting in front of me. I walked next to Dad and felt my heavy medal swinging under my jacket and my huge wad of gum balls in my mouth, and I felt warm and happy.

Eyes on the Prize

That Monday, during independent reading time, Miss Mabel called me, Cora, Minnie, and Matt to her desk.

"I have some reeeeeeeally exciting news," she said with a smile.

"We're going to Disneyland?" I guessed.

Whenever anyone has exciting news, that is always my first guess.

"Uhhhh . . . no," she said.

Figures. That guess is never right.

"At the 100 Days gallery, your project caught the attention of the Parents' Association," she explained. "They found the petition very persuasive. And this morning, the PA president gave me this."

She opened her desk drawer and pulled out a little gray-and-black rectangle.

"Holy cannoli," I said. "A speaker!"

The Fix-It Friends

Miss Mabel tapped her phone a few times, and all of a sudden, "Rama Lama Ding Dong" rang out of the speaker.

"Who wants to doo-wop?" Miss Mabel asked the class.

Everyone did, naturally.

It was our best doo-wop ever.

Take the Fix-It Friends Pledge!

I, (say your full name), do solemnly vow to help kids with their problems. I promise to be kind with my words and actions. I will try to help very annoying brothers even though they probably won't ever need help because they're soooooo perfect. Cross my heart, hope to cry, eat a gross old garbage fly.

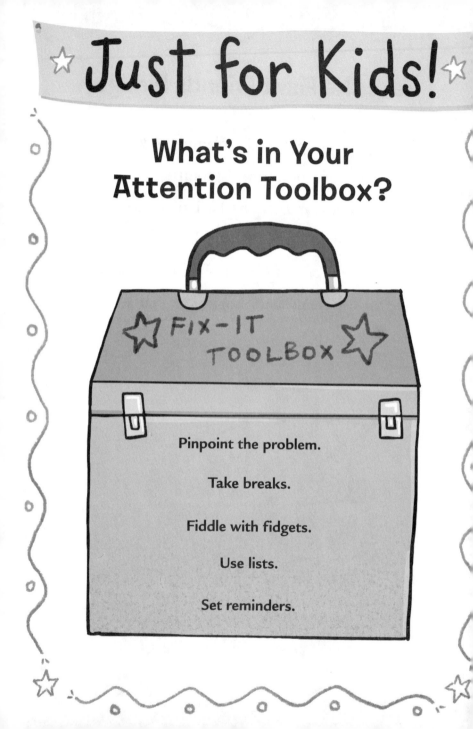

When Distraction Gets You Down . . .

Picture this:

You're in class, and your teacher's going on and on about some spelling rule that's so boring, you're about to fall asleep. Then you see a cool spider crawling on the windowsill. Maybe you run over to look, or you point it out to a friend, or maybe you watch it from your seat really, really closely. Then all of a sudden, your teacher's saying your name. You realize she just asked you a question, and you completely missed it. "Pay attention!" your teacher scolds. You gulp and nod, but really you're thinking, *I can't help it!*

Sound familiar? Hey, we've all been there.

How does it feel when you're distracted?

"It's like my brain is a hiker, and it's getting lost in the woods."

—Giovanni, age eleven

"I think, *I need to work*, but I can't do my work. If it was a video game, I'd use a power-up to get more strength and fight the distractions."

—Liam, age eight

"It feels sort of like if you wore hearing aids and they got knocked off—like the only thing you can hear is your mind talking."

—Stella, age nine

"My eyes go to other stuff in the classroom, and I start thinking about that, or somebody says something that reminds me of a TV show, and then I have no idea what just happened, and I am completely lost and kind of nervous."

—Kora, age twelve

What helps you pay attention?

"Sometimes if I'm distracting myself in class, my teacher lets me take a break and walk around the hall. When I go back to class, I'm more focused."
—Liam, age eight

"I cuddle my dog, Cider, and it helps me relax and focus."
—Sean, age nine

"A trick I learned is that if you constantly follow your teacher with your eyes, it helps you stay on track."
—Giovanni, age eleven

"If you don't sleep, then you won't be able to do anything without getting distracted, so I recommend sleeping at night."
—Kevin, age eleven

What to Do When It's Hard to Pay Attention

Getting distracted can get in your way and can make you feel really frustrated—especially if other people think you're goofing off when you're trying your best. Here's the thing: It's not your fault. Some people (grown-ups included) just have a harder time staying focused, keeping organized, and planning stuff.

News flash! Everyone has strengths and weaknesses. Even the most perfectly perfect person on the planet has stuff that's hard for him or her to do, and even the folks who seem to always be making mistakes have natural strengths and awesome talents.

Ever hear of a guy named Michael Phelps? He won twenty-eight Olympic medals for swimming. How about Simone Biles? She's a gymnast who nabbed four gold medals in her first Olympics, at age nineteen. What about Jim Carrey, Hollywood star, or Adam Levine, lead singer of the band Maroon 5? Or billionaire businessman Sir Richard Branson?

Know what they all have in common? As kids, all of them had a really hard time sitting still and paying attention. School was often really boring for them, and they struggled with it. It sure didn't stop them from taking the world by storm, did it?

Take a minute and think of three of your strengths—go ahead, I'll wait. . . . Got 'em? Maybe you have an amazing memory or a killer sense of humor or incredible balance, or maybe you're a master builder or a born leader or a whiz at languages or the backstroke or ventriloquism. *Raaaaaaahhh!* (That's the roar of the crowd cheering for you.) You're awesome!

Okay, now let's look at the skills that need work. Still with me? Cool!

Your brain's sort of like a control room, and in that room, there's a big, important control panel where the Big Bosses sit. It's the "Get Stuff Done" part of your brain (also known as the executive functions). It's the part that makes sure you pay attention, stay organized, remember stuff, control your impulses, and all sorts of other things. Some of the Big Bosses that work on this control panel are totally nailing their job, and some of them aren't doing their job as well as they should be. They just need extra training and practice to improve.

How can you improve those skills, so you're not quite as distracted?

So glad you asked!

1. Pinpoint the problem.

At first, it might seem like *all* of school is boring and you *always* have a hard time focusing or remembering stuff. But it's probably not really *all* or *always*. Ask yourself, *When is it hardest for me to pay attention? Which part of my day is giving me the most trouble or stressing me out?*

So if you absolutely hate homework, ask yourself, *Which part do I dread the most?* Maybe it's getting started, or maybe it's finishing up. Maybe it's the writing or the word problems in math.

Once you pinpoint the problem, it's way easier to find a solution. Here are a few solutions for some of the most common problems that pop up when it's hard to pay attention.

For when you're bored stiff

2. Fiddle with fidgets.

Some people learn best when their bodies are moving; it keeps their brains from falling asleep. Now, you can't shoot hoops or do backflips in class, but that's okay; small movements perk up your brain, too. Talk with your teacher about using a fidget—a small device that you move with your hands—just keep it quiet and on your lap, so it doesn't distract the other students. If the first kind you try doesn't help, try a different type—there are tons to choose from!

3. Take a break.

Ever been on a long hike and felt like you couldn't take another step? You probably took a little break, drank some water, and felt ready to hit the trails again in no time. Well, our brains get tired, too, especially if the work's hard. If you're having a tough time paying attention, ask your teacher or parents if you can take a little break. Just keep it short (three minutes or less), and make it active (do jumping jacks or walk to the water fountain).

For when you forget

4. Use lists.

If you keep forgetting things you need regularly, like your homework or your soccer cleats, your brain is telling you, *Dude! How 'bout a little help here?* What you need is a list! Keep it short, and hang it somewhere you can't miss it: on the front door, your planner, or a suitcase tag hanging off your backpack. Once you get used to seeing it there, move it to a new location.

5. Set reminders.

Are you fed up with hearing your parents nag you to study for your math quiz or make your bed? Replace them with robots! Reminders you set up yourself are a lot less annoying (and make you more independent). Program a watch to beep or vibrate, set an iPod to deliver a message, or just stick a Post-it on your fridge or bedroom door.

None of these strategies is magic, of course. It'll take time and practice to make those skills stronger. You'll mess up. It's kind of what we humans do. You'll forget stuff and daydream and lose your patience. And when you do, you'll tell yourself, *No big deal. I'll just try again.*

Keep on trying. Be kind to yourself. The sky's the limit, so let yourself fly high.

Want more tips or fixes for other problems? Just want to check out some Fix-it Friends games and activities? Visit the Fix-It Friends website at fixitfriendsbooks.com!

Resources for Parents

If your child struggles with planning, attention, and organization, you may find these resources helpful.

Books for Kids

A Bird's-Eye View of Life with ADD and ADHD, 3rd edition, by Chris A. Zeigler Dendy and Alex Zeigler, Chris A. Zeigler Dendy Consulting LLC, 2015

Cory Stories: A Kid's Book About Living with ADHD by Jeanne Krauss, Magination Press, 2004

Learning to Slow Down and Pay Attention: A Book for Kids About ADHD, 3rd edition, by Kathleen G. Nadeau and Ellen B. Dixon, Magination Press, 2004

The Lightning Thief (Percy Jackson and the Olympians, Book 1) by Rick Riordan, Hyperion, 2005

My Friend the Troublemaker: Learning to Focus and Thriving with ADHD by Rifka Schonfeld, Philipp Feldheim, 2012

Putting on the Brakes: Understanding and Taking Control of Your ADD or ADHD, 3rd edition, by Patricia O. Quinn and Judith M. Stern, Magination, 2012

Books for Parents

8 Keys to Parenting Children with ADHD by Cindy Goldrich, W. W. Norton & Company, 2015

Driven to Distraction (Revised): Recognizing and Coping with Attention Deficit Disorder by Edward M. Hallowell and John J. Ratey, Anchor, 2011

Ready, Set, Breathe: Practice Mindfulness with Your Children for Fewer Meltdowns and a More Peaceful Family by Carla Naumberg, New Harbinger, 2015

Smart but Scattered: The Revolutionary "Executive Skills" Approach to Helping Kids Reach Their Potential by Peg Dawson and Richard Guare, Guilford Press, 2009

Taking Charge of ADHD: Third Edition: The Complete, Authoritative Guide for Parents by Russell A. Barkley, The Guilford Press, 2013

Understanding Girls with ADHD: How They Feel and Why They Do What They Do, 2nd edition, by Kathleen G. Nadeau, Ellen B. Littman, and Patricia O. Quinn, Advantage Books, 2015

Websites

ADD Resources

www.addresources.org

CHADD

www.chadd.org

PTS Coaching

www.ptscoaching.com

Understood

www.understood.org

About the Author

Nicole C. Kear grew up in New York City, where she still lives with her husband, three firecracker kids, and a ridiculously fluffy hamster. She's written lots of essays and a memoir, *Now I See You*, for grown-ups, and she's thrilled to be writing for kids, who make her think hard and laugh harder. She has a bunch of fancy, boring diplomas and one red clown nose from circus school. Seriously.

nicolekear.com